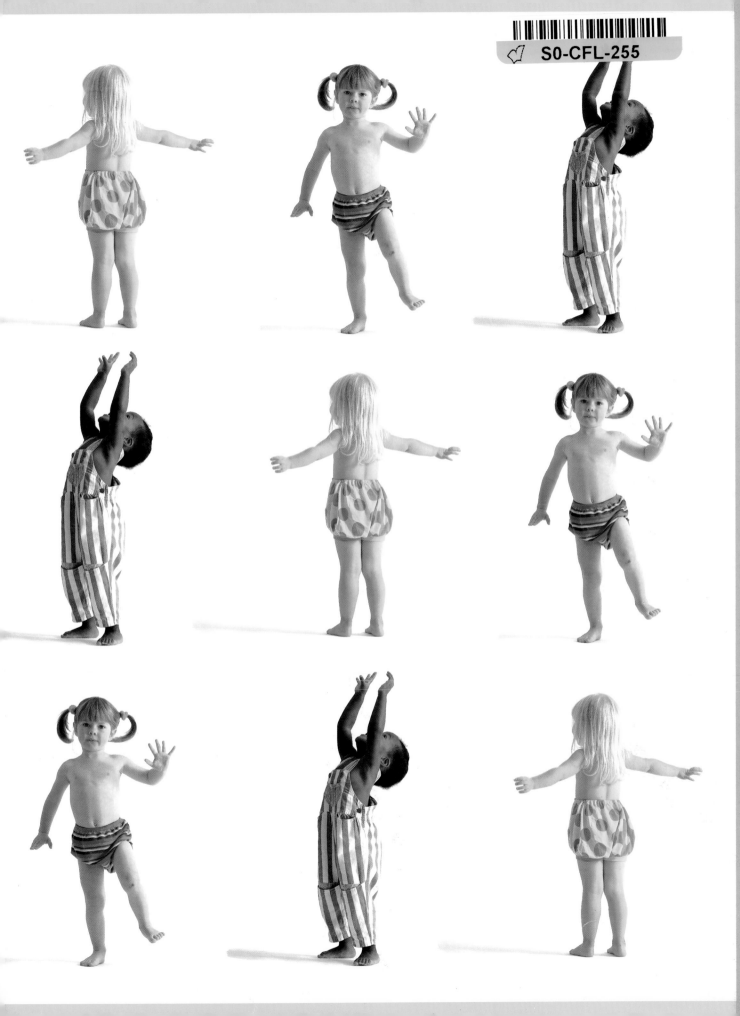

for Dora and Jack – D.M.
for Alan – A.S.

First edition for the United States, Canada, and
the Philippines published 1994 by Barron's Educational Series, Inc.

**all about ME** copyright © Frances Lincoln Limited 1994
Text copyright © Debbie MacKinnon 1994
Illustrations copyright © Anthea Sieveking 1994

First published in Great Britain in 1994 by Frances Lincoln Ltd

*All inquiries should be addressed to:*
Barron's Educational Series, Inc.
250 Wireless Boulevard
Hauppauge, NY 11788

International Standard Book No. 0-8120-6348-1
Library of Congress Catalog Card No. 93-23143

**Library of Congress Cataloging-in-Publication Data**
MacKinnon, Debbie.
   All about me / Debbie MacKinnon: photographs by Anthea Sieveking.
   — 1st ed. in U.S.
      p.   cm.
   Summary: Photographs show children of different ethnic backgrounds
pointing out the parts of their body and using them in a variety of ways.
   ISBN 0-8120-6348-1
   1. Body, Human—Juvenile literature.   [1. Body, Human.]
I. Sieveking, Anthea, ill.   II. Title.
QM27, M33 1994
612—dc20                                                    93–23143
                                                             CIP
                                                             AC

Printed and bound in Hong Kong

4567  9870  987654321

# all about
# ME

Debbie MacKinnon
Photographs by Anthea Sieveking

BARRON'S

# My body

Can you stretch right out like Kelly?

# Now point to all the parts of her body.

- head
- back
- shoulder
- chest
- arm
- leg
- tummy
- hair
- knee
- bottom
- fingers
- toes
- face
- wrist
- ankle
- hand
- foot
- elbow
- eye
- nose
- mouth

Can you find all these parts on your own body?

# My face

Can you point to all these parts?
• eyes • ears • mouth • nose
• eyelashes • eyebrows
• lips • teeth • chin
• cheeks • forehead

# My hair

Isabel has fair, curly hair.

Rosie has long, thick hair.

Christopher has dark, straight hair.

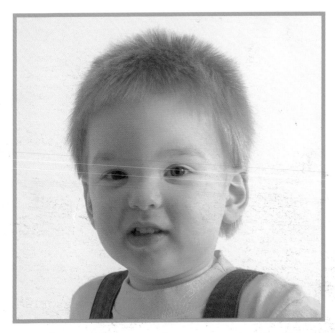

Joshua has short, spiky hair.

What kind of hair do you have?

# My hands

Are your hands as big as Hannah's?
Put your hands on top of hers. Now
count your fingers.

Christopher needs both hands to pick up big teddy.

Jim likes pressing the buttons on the phone with his finger.

Elliot holds out his hand to catch the bubble.

Levi picks up a pea with his finger and thumb.

What else can you do with your hands?

# My feet

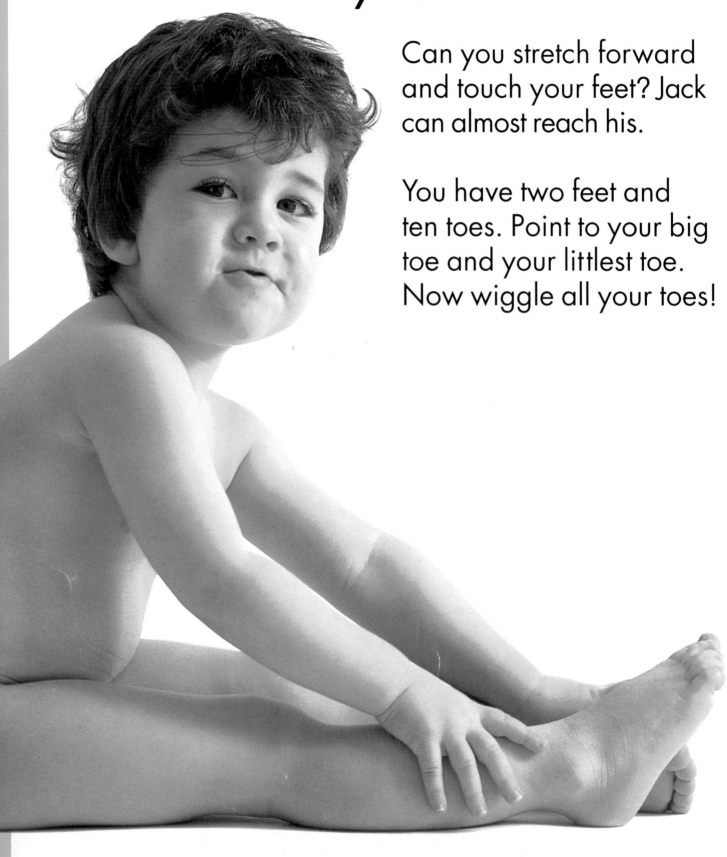

Can you stretch forward and touch your feet? Jack can almost reach his.

You have two feet and ten toes. Point to your big toe and your littlest toe. Now wiggle all your toes!

Kelly balances
on tip-toe.

Ann walks along
the plank, without
falling off!

Katherine pushes
with her feet,
and scoots
along on
her bike.

Rosie jumps up and
down on the trampoline.

What else can you do with your feet?

# My ears, eyes, nose, and mouth

Joshua likes cooking.
Here he is calling Laura to
come and try a freshly
baked cookie.

Laura can hear Joshua
with her ears.

Laura can see the cookie with her eyes.

Now she can smell it with her nose,

and she can taste the cookie with her tongue. Yummy!

Careful, it might still be hot!

What else do you like to taste?

# My skin

Your skin covers your whole body. Daniel has fallen over, and skinned his knees. Now he has two bandages while he waits for new skin to grow underneath. Daniel likes his bandages!

You can touch and feel with your skin.

Miriam's new sweater feels rough and scratchy.

Christopher's rabbit feels soft and furry.

Jessica's ball feels
smooth and round.

The water in Isabel's
pool feels cold and wet...

...but Isabel's towel
feels warm and dry.

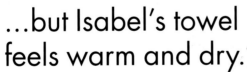

Touch Mommy's face.
Now touch Daddy's face.
How do they feel?

# Taking care of my body

Your body gets dirty every day.

Mark has found his big sister's chocolate, so he really needs a good washing!

It's bath time...

Now Mark is clean again and Kelly is having a shampoo. Can you wash yourself?

Teeth need cleaning too —
Ann is brushing hers.

Now Ann's teeth are
white and shiny.

Mommy is cutting Jack's fingernails.
Snip, snip, snip — it doesn't hurt.
Don't forget the toenails!

# How many?

What a lot of parts in your body.
Can you count them?

**1** head •tummy •nose •mouth •tongue •neck
**2** eyes •ears •arms •hands •legs •feet •cheeks
**10** fingers •toes •fingernails •toenails
**20** teeth (have you got them all yet?)
and don't forget **1,000s** of hairs on your head!

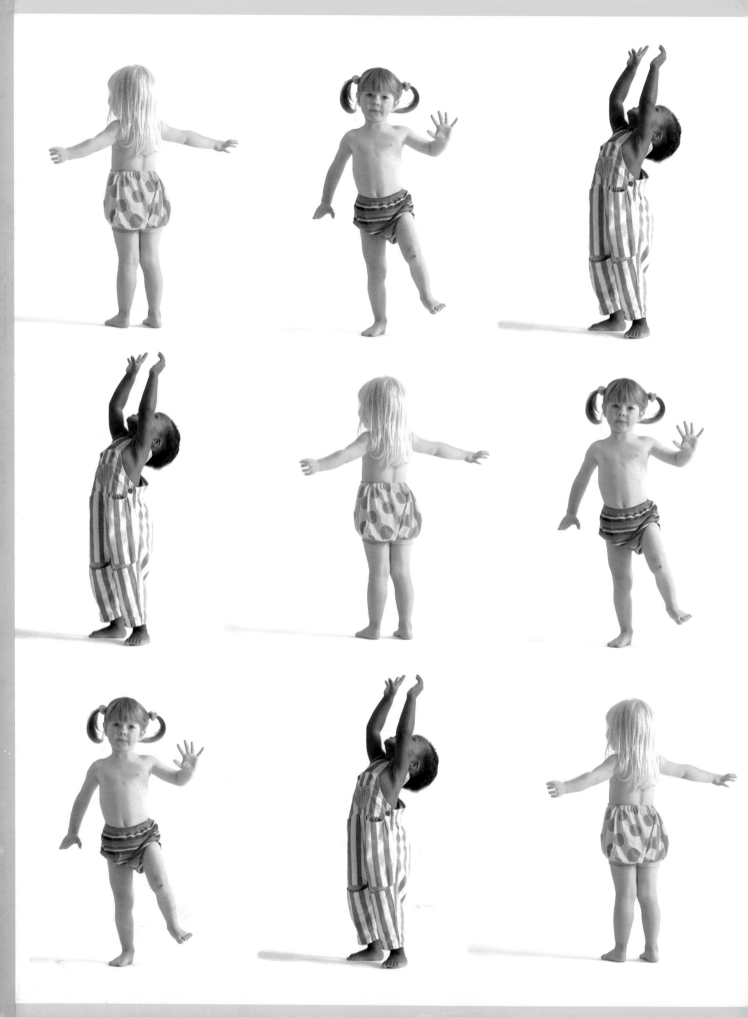